The thing was when I was there then I just

disappeared to a different reality and then I

just come back two days before I would have

graduated and then I realized I was in a bad

dream then you could have never had thought

about what had happened next I was the living

man with a gift from above. What it was like

there it was like the start and finish of

anything you want to do and it was all done it

was the short cut to anything I wanted but all I

had to do was put into this reality and then I

could do anything I want and life was going to

be so fun I was so excited that I figured out

how to put together something that no one

could have never done and then I could be the

one that had the time other people's life. It was

perfect but when little Lou woke he was stuck

in his small apartment and it didn't came as

easy has he had done in his dreams he thought

really hard the next day he thought he would

be the best in the world at anything and all he

had to was spend the time and pursue how to

a famous rockstar but he realized that he

didn't know how to but he began to start

crying that he didn't have really anything

other then rent money and his bus pass that he

really need to survive but he didn't really care

about the money all he want was to be famous

and have people that care about him like in a

fairy tail that end up killing themself and all of

there people but this was a weird day he start

the day at three in the morning and starting

beer a lot of water and thought to be a glass

world drinking champion but he then fell over

his bed and die that when nick and his fellows

had broken in and had kill him nick and his

friends work for a group of people that didn't

have the right amount of time to let silly and

stupid people have fun and he was a problem

to other people and someone put money on his

head to kill him nick went home that night and

got a phone call that he done a good job and he

would love to see him on different and more

jobs but nick didn't really have the option to

stop what he was doing he wonder if he could

have done something different in life but he

didn't really like do hard labor or just hard

work anyway nick had ten friends from high

school two strippers and three homies that he

would smoke cigars with he didn't really have

the moral of having girlfriends since his

mother an father got a divorce and he always

thought to be since because he know that he

didn't find the right women for him that would

be all about his life and what he does but he

did have girlfriend but nothing to special just

one night stands and would do other things

with them but he didn't really like the outcome

of his last job since he had to do it with people

he didn't really know or trust but he didn't

really care anymore about keeping his

freedom he was just in it for the money and he

didn't really want to go to jail but he didn't

have no way to go to job so then the next day

after nick party all night he got a phone call

from his mom and she was telling him that

they are have a birthday party for his aunt

Kelly and she was turning fifty one and she

want to have all of her family and friends there

for she could see them again and she didn't

want anyone skipping out she if they didn't go

then she would stop send Christmas cards and

family photos to all who didn't came and the

nick said well I be there then can't miss out on

a family get to together. He then asked what

day is and what time then nick got a knock on

the door and then he open it and it was just the

mailmen just delivering the mail and he hung

and ran to his car not locking the door half-

dressed and then he began to drive till he

forgot his package, the package was a special

knife that a European city use to cut peoples

body parts off after they stole or did

something so bad that they had to get

punished. Then the day nick woke up all mess

up after a long and terrible night that he

couldn't remember he woke up in his car two

city's over in a city called Williamsburg that's

when nick realized that he had to be home to

get ready for his aunt's party. The drive home

was a long thirty-minute drive and nick was

looking in the mirror and he realized that he

was hurt and had black eyes and was bruised

on his face. When nick saw that he try to

remember but nothing came to him and all he

could do was drive he end up getting pull over

and the police officer came up to his car and

ask what had happened and then nick said bar

flight and I stayed at my buddies house and

just woke up the officer ask if he know how

fasted he was going nick then said I'm running

late to a birthday party that I need to be going

to. The police gave him his license back after

he had sat there for ten minutes while the

police officer went back to his car nick then

drive away and then nick got into a car

accident after another car hit him in the back

end of his car. The other car looked beat up

and couldn't go anyway nick then drive away

out of fear that something bad was about to

happen to him nick was trying to realize what

was going to happen to him he thought that

someone or even the police were after him he

thought again and end up driving to his safe

house three city's west of where his house

was. He got to the city of the royal city and he

realized that nothing bad was going to happen

as long as he got to his gun safe but nick didn't

lose his cell phone and he couldn't believe this

was happening to him but he didn't have

anyone that follows him so there was nothing

up is what nick had thought but then he got to

his safe house and his home was gone through

and all of the things were missing and he had

to put together who had just killed to pinpoint

who was coming after him and what they want

to him. After all, he didn't go there unless he

needs guns money, or a place to hide away

from his family but he was confused and was

losing hope that he didn't have a last-ending

mission in him. Nick wasn't trained by the

government or any flight or killing group how

he learns to kill flight people was that he had a

serious accident that made him almost die and

it gave him the images to not feel bad for

people that didn't do anything for him the only

thing was that he didn't have the money to be

hunted by the mobs and gangs to be flighting

in the streets about who gets the streets. How

nick got his money he would work at a store

that would sell pets like cats and dogs fish and

different kinds of spiders. It didn't pay that

much but enough to pay guns armor ammo

and food rent and he gave his safe house from

his father's house. But the house wasn't gone

through like how you would think how nick

know was that he had a spy pen that would

always record what's was inside the living

room and that when he caught three masked

men going through his house. The masked

man was wearing bark cloths and look like

there were upset that they didn't find anything

that they need to put nick into jail and that's

when Nick got to his room and got his back up

cell phone it was an old phone that was a flip

phone that cost him twenty bucks a month and

it may have just pay off for him to use. Nick

was so upset that he was about to go to jail it

all came to him while he reaches over his desk

and that's when his phone rang that no know

ever call other than spam and scammers and

nick never call anybody but and didn't gave his

number out. The phone was only for getting

out of town and that's when Nick didn't

answer and it rang and rang and rang but nick

never answer and he didn't think anything

about it but nick needs to make a call to an old

bookie that he would place wagers with but

why he needs to talk to an old bookie was nick

need money to get out of the country and after

time he could come back to the United States

but where he wants to go was any way to keep

his freedom. So he gave Tony a call and Tony

answer and ask who was it he then nick ask

you let me borrow ten k. Tony said to nick that

he can't be giving him money to never see him

again but then Nick said yeah I know you can't

but I think I could wire transfer money back to

in time I'll pay five extra thousand for you

make something on it and everyone happy and

on there way. Okay, I can do it but I better get

my money! Okay, you will just have to wait a

couple of days weeks just need some time

away from the USA. Okay, I got you my friend

but can you come pick it up I'll leave it outside

my car inside of the dash that where it will be

and I hope you know I'll get my money I'll

come to where you are and I'll find you naked

or die but until I get my money. No none of

that will happen but for real I will pay you just

trust me I never did you wrong and I never

will I got people that would pay it off for me if

they know so you don't need to get upset

about anything and everything got to work out

just please help me out. Okay okay, I will when

you come and get the money. Here soon I'll

text you when I'm close. No need so it will be

today. Yes, I'm going to get into the shower

and eat some white noodles and then be over

there okay goodbye. Nick then went got into

the shower and fell into the tub and start

taking a bath then nick went downstair call

and order and white noodle from a little

Chinese place that was famous for being dirty

and cheap but nick like the restaurant because

they always gave free white rice and was

always a some hot Chinese teen that was

always looking high with her bloodshot eyes.

But nick remembers that if the cops were after

him then they would have already been there

and got him and put him into jail but that's not

what happen so nick got his food and then

locked his safe house door and brought the

food with him to Tony house to get the money

on the way there nick was going a little fast he

was on a country road going down peach ave

and then turn on to bluefin and there he was at

Tony's and Nick left his car on the street And

left it running and run up to Tony's car and

that when a cop with his lights on was going so

fast that it made the road shake and Nick got in

Tony car and got the money. The money was in

a bank envelope with a sticky note on it and

the note said hello Nick I hope you know that

this money came from hard work and I'll see it

again ten or broken arms and legs. Then Nick

got out of the car ran back to his car and went

back home to his safe house. When nick got

back to his safe house nick realized that he had

to make a plan to get out of the country before

it was too late and that when Nick stays up all

night and got thinking on palaver about how to

get money how to work how to get friends

how to start over but that's when nick got a

message from his mom that he missed his aunt

birthday and she was mad at him forever but

nick never text back and he was upset that his

life was about to end but that when nick want

to start over anyway and he would love to

leave the country and forgot his family but he

didn't know where to go but he didn't want to

go alone so he stays up planing and crying that

his life was not working out and he would love

a chance to start over if it was given! But the

next day nick slept into the next night and

didn't get how to get out of the country unsee

and unheard but he began to think of how to

make a new idea for traveling but he was so

lost in ideals that he just put his mind back

into his pillow and turn on the old boxed

television and began to think of if all of his

ideas would just go away and that's when he

thought that he was in the clear because he did

go to jail yet and if the cops were after him

then he would already be in the courtroom

yelling my life is over and I will die in a prison

cell. But that wasn't the case and then he

thought that he missed his Aunt's birthday and

he would be in big money problems if he didn't

give the money back to his old bookie Tony but

nick had a lot of money and know no one know

where it was at. Nick had the money outside

his a big metal box outside in a wooden area.

He had it marked by different markers and he

was the only person that knows where it was

at so he went to the wooden area and got

about one hundred thousand in cash and nick

still had the ten thousand and what he did next

was he went to his casual home and went and

call Tony and said you should pick up your

money and if I can not pay you the next five

thousand that would be great Tony then said

no you made a deal and I need my money

anyway why are you not going out of the states

Tony said? Something came up and I need to

stay here! Okay, I'll be there in one hour but

you can keep the five thousand it's no big deal.

Okay, thanks it has only been two days and I

am thanking you from the bottom of my heart

that you did that for me. Well, it's no big deal

maybe start betting again then things would

be even better for me, we all know your not a

good gambler but I hope you're not losing your

mind and doing bad things that would hurt me

know you. No no I'm not I am not I just

thinking of a vacation. O well, it seems like you

in a hurry all the time well least when I talk to

you. No, come get your money back I'm busy

and I have to be getting ready for a dinner with

my date. O okay, see you when I get there. The

next four days nicks was to stay at his casual

place and call the cops on the break-in at his

other house. The cops show up and nick gave

them a report and said that they got it all on

camera but they were wearing masks. That's

when the police said that it is unusual for them

to be wearing masks. Can we see the video he

said it an app on my phone that shows it to me

but it was a little pen camera that I got online

when I was a teenager? Okay, I will have to

record it on my phone because there's no way

to get the video unless you can send it to me

but normal the pen camera not let you do it so

Nick look at his phone and try to send the cop

the video and it was no way of doing so so the

cop got his cell phone and start recording the

video. Then nick got back to what he was

planing and got a phone call for the nick hit he

had to kill a man that was terrible man that

was cheating on his two wife's and his boss

need him to do it right away but Nick was

unsure if he was the man for the job because of

how hard it was. They required nick to go out

of state and into a little town with a population

of two hundred and nick didn't want to be

noticed. So nick said give me a day and call me

back and I'll tell you I'm in with the job and

then you can tell him the details. Okay

goodbye yeah yeah later. That night nick stay

up late watching scary movies and had soda

and popcorn all over his rocking chair. Nick

fell asleep in his rocking chair and woke up to

a loud bang going off. It was only nine in the

morning and nick had heard a loud boom it

was coming from a burning home down the

street. Nick went and look and there were so

many fire trucks and police cars outside on his

block. Nick felt so happy that he wasn't in the

cop car that he got the nerves and was going to

do the job. So nick got in the shower and brush

his teeth and was about to get his bag packed

that's when he got the mail out of the mailbox

and it was a letter from the United state army

said that he couldn't travel outside the USA

because of a new deadly virus that was only in

European country's. Nick was weird out but it

didn't stop him nothing never really stop him

he just was a person that had no emotions. So

nick went back inside and was continued to

pack. He waits all day and then it was five o

clock he call his boss and he got no answer. So

nick made some kinds of rice and call it a night.

The next day nicks boss give him a call and

told him that the clip was a black man and he

wasn't sure who he was described but nick ask

him was his name and what the location was

and he said it's in Ohio in a town called welder

his name blank brooks and he is an unwanted

man that has two wife's and he owns a lot of

people a lot of money and he is a trucker he

had his only semi and he doesn't work he live

at 235 south apple street he lives in a tiny

white trailer with his first wife he doesn't have

any kids with his first wife but he has four with

his second wife and he is a loser to the heart

but he is up for do and we need you to

complete this order. Okay, I can do that it will

take a few days the drive will be about three

and half hours and I will hope to catch him out

and about. But if not I'll run-up inside the

trailer and wack him in front of his wife. Or

should we do it differently and have you help

me put together a plan. Well, I think you can

take him out by yourself but make sure there

are no police around! Okay will do that when

should I go and do that and how much will I

get paid? Anytime in the next year, you will see

and thirty thousand wow was so much you

will see how hard it is killing this person. He

already killed four of my man so be careful.

Okay, will do well with me luck okay goodbye

good luck and goodbye. The next day nick take

the night and slept in till about noon and got

his bag and get into his car and head to blank's

house. Nick drove for two hours stop and got

food at a gas station he got a slice of pizza and

some French fries and water and ate there at

the gas station where he noticed people

looking at him and starting wondering if they

were noticing him for his clothes or something

he said. He was sure and he got a bad feeling

that's when Nick went up to the group of

women and ask why are you looking at me for

the past ten minutes? The women's said we

can't just not noticed a loser like yourself! The

women started laughing and roughing their

hair. Nick said back your group of people are

just up to no good and I think one day you will

meet your maker and you will then see as Nick

started to laugh. Then it got very silent and the

group of women said let me guess you're a bad

man but to know just like we learn at church

that's how we know you're not even from

around here. Then Nick said if he could sit with

them and the women said no you should eat by

yourself because I hate when strangers need

things especially stranger up to no good, like

sorry your cutie and that's not how you pull

women then nick said o sorry I thought you

were up to no good and I just don't get in with

a lot of people I don't get out much too. Sorry

anyway, I hope I'm not worrying you I'm just

not from away here I noticed that you guys

were looking and laughing at me so I thought I

just made sure we were all good. Well, we are

now as some women start to tear up! Then

nick and sat back down and then began eating

again. Then the gas station manager came over

to nick and ask what was he doing talking to

those women because they just ran out and

they are for real a bad group and they are

really up to bad things so you better watch

yourself I was watching you right behind the

counter. Then Nick said I got it to trust me I am

not scared of a bunch of girls that never grow

up and are stuck in a little town. People that

never got the message that they are unwanted

and wash up are people like the women. The

gas station manager said s right well you need

to be getting out of here Mr. I don't need to

hear someone that just as bad. Nick said can I

eat? Sure but make it fast and I mean in a

hurry. Okay okay, then nick sat there looking

at the clock on the wall and then ate his slice of

pizza and then got up to use the restroom, and

then a man and black mask came in and said

out the money in the bag! Nick ran to the

restroom and locked the door. The next thing

that happen was the masked man banged on

the door and nick told him that no one was in

here. So the Masked man told Nick that I'm not

going to hurt you then nick heard gunshots

and blood leak through the door and nick was

scared that he was going to die. Nick only had

a pocket knife on him they was a big as his

middle finger and it was no match for a

gunman that allowed hurt people over money

that the masked man could have just got the

money and ran out of the gas station but

instead Nick was locked in the restroom and

he was in there for about five minutes and

then he got his cell phone out going through

shock he calls nine one one. Then the cop on

the other line asked if he was okay and why

did he call and then nick said because I'm at a

gas station and I'm locked in the restroom and

there is a masked man that's got a gun and

there is blood on the floor leaking in. Okay, I'll

send swat, and all of the men that are in the

area just hold tight stay on the phone with me

I'll be your lifeline you will make it just trust

me! Nick said okay and then his phone alert

said his phone running dead and is about to

die Nick then tells the cop that his phone might

die and if he doesn't make it to my mother and

father that I love them. Then nick heard the

cops lights under the door and heard their

sirens and nick realized that the masked man

tells him to open up that he wasn't there and

nick almost opens the door then the cop on the

phone tells him that the man is on the gas

station still and he's got to hurt you because

his life is over and he doesn't want you to

remember any of this. Nicks's phone dies and

the cops enter the gas station then guns shot

are fired then one office said man down calling

all other units. Then the police break down the

door and nick is standing here with his knife

nick would not let anyone in so the police had

to break it down. That's when nick was so

scared that the police were going to take him

to the hospital and make sure he was okay but

that when nick started talking to the cop and

told him that he was fine no need for the other

bill and the cop let Nick going on his way after

about an hour in the back of an ambulance

while he was there they checked his eyes and

his ears and heartbeat and veins. To make sure

that he wasn't in shock or anything that nick

wasn't telling the paramedic. So nick drove to

the next rest stop it was a ten-minute ride on

the highway four but he didn't care anymore

what had just happened to him was so crazy

that he could yell till he lost his voice. But nick

had to go over the direction on the map and he

had printed them out at his house but he didn't

know exactly how far away he was until he

looked at the map. So he looks at it and what

he found was that he was in the wrong town

but he wasn't far he didn't know exactly how

far but he was about to look it up on his smart

cell phone. To that what he did he type in 235

south apple street Ohio and it told him that he

was exactly twenty-five miles from the

location and nick then got excited about how

he was about to get paid and go home and tell

his mom what had happened at the gas

station! So then nick slept in his car till early

morning and then took off. He got to the town

of Welder and stop and got his gun out of his

bag and there was a firework shop in the

middle of welder so nick thought after he

would get some fireworks and let them off

when he got home. So while nick was driving

he spotted a chicken restaurant called Mary

chicken club and he was hungry so he thought

to stop but before that, he had to get the job

done. So Nick went to 235 south apple street

and that just what he did. Nick got there and

then he got out of the car and there was no

knowledge insight but then he grabs his bag

and put his gun in front his pants and walk to

the door he then got to the door and knocked.

Then a man came to the door it was Blanko

brooks then nick asks him to come outside to

his car Nick then explain that he was selling

tickets for his community and the tickets were

for coupons on gas and oil changes and that

they never expired then nick said that he was

from a couple towns over and he need your

money to make him a better person and make

him a leader in his community! Then Blanko

said sure how much they cost? Nick then said

you know what I'll buy them for you and you

can just have them but we need to go to my car

or let me go grab them okay? Then Blanko said

sure I'll walk over there that's when Nick shot

him in the legs than the arms then Blanko was

crying and ask why he was doing this then

Nick shot him in the head and then Nick got

back in his car and drove home and call his

boss and said that the job was done. Nick

never got fireworks and was upset that he

didn't so he thought he would have to get

someone day but that's when his boss call and

told him that he got another job for him and he

need to meet him for that he can pay him. So

nick went and meet his boss and got paid and

then got a letter and a yellow folder with

information on the next hit. Nick didn't want

to kill people anyone he got the last big payday

and decided to come work for his boss and

have the dream job of getting fast money and

get paid. The worst thing nick could have

thought about when he would work for his

boss it was sometimes long drives and long

late hours of scary thoughts and feelings about

who and what they did to get hurt! Nick had

decided to go home after talking with his boss

for short minutes nick wasn't excited to

explore the country but nick had a feeling that

he was about to travel a lot more and he was

not that happy that he was going to go to work

but if he got some much money that he never

had to go to work then he could go and do it

but he only had five hundred in his bank

account and the last payment for the hit, he

didn't want to consider that he one day he

would die but he didn't fear death and wasn't

scary to die but he wants to live a happy and

glad and cheerful life so when he would think

of his work it didn't make sense that he work

where he did. So the next night nick began to

look in the folder and it was a hit list of more

then ten people. The list was from young men

and women to old people that haven't seen the

day light in a couple of years. So nick grab his

cell phone and call his boss and ask how much

would this pay for all ten and he his boss said

twenty thousand there all local and they are all

in trouble with the government and local

police so we are helping them out but what

they would do was put them in jail and that

not what they need to do nick so if you don't

do it then you don't get paid and I'll fine

someone else and there all family so it won't

be hard to locate them. All you got to do is

kidnap one of them and tell them to tell them

where all the other lives. So nick hung up

because his phone dead and he was unsure if

he could pull it off because his boss didn't

know where some of them live! But thought

that they were around on earth so it couldn't

be that hard he thought to put up missing

poster but that would get him in trouble but

Nick was the type of guy that he just didn't

care until he got what he wanted. The next day

nick look the names on the internet and he

find where they live though a website that he

paid to look at phone records date of birthdays

and places where they live. So nick showed up

at a party and all ten people where there

drinking and having a good time. The thing

was nick was uninvited and was not supposed

to be there by nick didn't care. The party had a

lot of people there and when nick fried the

first shot hitting billy then silly then people

start to run and yell that he's got a gun. The

party got shot up and all of all the other people

he need to kill was hiding in the basement and

they had the door locked. When nick got to the

basement he try opening the door but he

couldn't so he shot the door open and then he

kill all the people down in the basement. As he

walked up the steps he wish that the other

people that didn't do anything were not down

there but nick thought that he had to do what

he had to do and he was not stop till he got

paid. So leave the party nick stole a bottom of

whiskey and couple beers and the. He got into

his car and left. As he got into the car. He

noticed that he's car had been gone through

and he was upset that someone had look

through his car but he start the car and flown

home. That when nick got a phone call from

his mother and what his mother said was that

she was sorry and that he had she had fail him

and his life she mean more then what it is and

she would love if Nick would came over for

some tea and sandwich's on Saturday then

Nick said maybe nothings wrong everything

fines you did your best. So nick hung up and

then call his boss and told him that the job was

done and he would like to get paid that when

his boss told him that he would love if you

would like to eat dinner with me and some of

my family and then I can paid you then Nick

said sure my mom wants to have lunch on

Saturday what day is it? Nicks boss then said

it's on Friday night out of town at a steak

house. The first thing that came into Nick's

mind was that his boss was going to hurt or

even more kill him for he could take all his

money back and laugh at him, but it didn't

seem like Nicks boss wanted to hurt him, but

Nick was unsure, so he didn't want that to

happen to him, so he said yeah I'll make it

what time? Nicks Boss then said seven o clock

at The only steak house in Indian county. Nick

said ok can you pay me for that one thing?

Nicks boss said yeah I got you no problem.

Then nick went to the dinner and got his

money and didn't say anything to his boss and

left.